For Fiona, Jake, Ben, and Isaac

Text copyright © Jonny Zucker, 2007
Illustrations copyright © Ned Woodman, 2007
Houdini photo copyright © Topfoto

"Mission 1: Game On" was originally published in English in 2007. This edition is published by an arrangement with STRIPES PUBLISHING, an imprint of Magi Publications.

Darby Creek
A division of Lerner Publishing Group, Inc.
241 First Avenue North
Minneapolis, MN 55401 U.S.A.

Website address: www.lernerbooks.com

Library of Congress Cataloging-in-Publication Data

Zucker, Jonny.
Game on / by Jonny Zucker ; illustrated by Ned Woodman.
    pages   cm. — (Max Flash ; mission 1)
Originally published in the United Kingdom by Stripes Publishing, 2007.
Summary: "When the top secret Department for Extraordinary Activity discovers that an evil computer game character has escaped from the Virtual world and is intent on causing chaos, they know the time has come for Max's first mission. There are dangerous monsters to fight and a perilous plot to foil. Does Max have the special skills needed to save the day?"— Provided by publisher.
    ISBN 978-1-4677-1207-1 (lib. bdg. : alk. paper)
    ISBN 978-1-4677-2051-9 (eBook)
 [1. Computer games—Fiction. 2. Virtual reality—Fiction. 3. Monsters—Fiction.
4. Adventure and adventurers—Fiction.] I. Woodman, Ned, 1978– illustrator. II. Title.
                    PZ7.Z77925Gam 2013
   [Fic]—dc23   2012049019

Manufactured in the United States of America
1 – BP – 7/15/13

MAX FLASH
MISSION 1

GAME ON

Jonny Zucker

Illustrated by
Ned Woodman

MAX FLASH
MISSION 1

CHAPTER 1

Max Flash was desperate. He struggled with the metal chains wrapped around his upper body. They dug into his ribs. They pinched at his back. Water gushed all around him. It was up to his waist and rising fast. He had to get out of here in the next minute. Or his whole body would be underwater.

He twisted to the left. He twisted to the right. One of the chains uncoiled and fell into the water. He allowed himself a tiny spark of satisfaction. But still the water rose. It was

MAX FLASH

halfway up his chest. He yanked his right
elbow backwards. Another chain came free. He
tried the same move with his left elbow. The
chain remained in place. He cursed under his
breath. He slammed his left fist forward and
backward. The third chain slipped off.

The water continued its rapid rise. It swept against his chin.

Come on, come on! Get the fourth chain off!

A drop of water trickled into his mouth. Max spat it out. He shook his body. He brought his elbows crashing together. The final chain came off. Water started to go up his nostrils. Max reached out and grabbed the ledge above him. He dragged himself upward and scrambled out of the tank. He landed on the hard wooden floor with a squelchy thud.

He bent over and rested the palms of his hands on his thighs. He tried to catch his breath.

"Pretty good!" said Max's dad as he walked toward him. His dad turned off the tap that had been flooding the tank with water. "But it was a close call. You could do with being five seconds faster."

CHAPTER 2

Max's parents were stage magicians.
Montgomery and Carly Flash had been
performing their magic act for more than
twenty years. Montgomery's stage name
was the Great Montello. Carly was known as
Mystical Cariba. They were both extremely
good illusionists. Their magic took in even the
most hardened cynics.

Max had grown up backstage. He had
watched his parents perform. He also saw a
lot of other magic acts. He'd been fascinated

by their dazzling tricks. He figured out how they worked. He tried them out himself. He practiced and practiced until he got them perfect.

But Max wasn't just good at doing magic tricks. He had been born with a rare double-jointedness. His body was remarkably flexible and bendy. He could slide through the narrow park railings. He was never found during hide-and-seek because he could hide in impossibly tiny spaces.

He had remarkable physical traits and dedication. These things had made him a first-class escape artist, contortionist, and illusionist.

So being tied up in chains and escaping from a tank of water was nothing out of the ordinary. This trick was a new part of the stage act. It was based on a trick done by Harry Houdini, Max's all-time hero.

Max changed out of his wet clothes. He

sauntered into the living room. The now-empty tank stood in the corner. His parents were by the window having a hushed conversation.

"Er, excuse me," Max announced. "Are you going to let me in on the secret?"

His mom and dad spun around. They both looked on edge.

"What's going on?" Max demanded.

His dad gave him a guilty smile.

"There's something we need to show you," said his mom.

Max watched as they walked out of the room. His mom unbolted the door that led to the cellar.

Max frowned.

His parents hardly ever went down to the cellar. It was dark and cramped.

"Don't worry," said his dad with a reassuring smile. "There's nothing to be afraid of."

Max reached the cellar. His eyes adjusted to the dim light. He could just see old paint cans, mounds of yellowing newspapers, and bits of an old motorbike strewn about.

He watched his dad walk over to the wooden workbench by the far wall. He felt for something behind it. To Max's surprise, the workbench began to move slowly.

It swiveled open ninety degrees. It stopped when it was pressed against the wall. His dad walked over to the space where the bench had been. He slid open a panel on the floor.

"Er, is this part of a new trick?" asked Max. His eyes were wide with surprise. "Because if it is, it looks pretty cool."

His mom shook her head. "Come and see for yourself," she said.

Max watched. First his dad and then his mom lowered themselves through the opening. They climbed down a metal ladder. Max walked over. He stared through the opening. It was so dark. He could just make out the shapes of his parents. Where did these steps lead? What was down there?

He hesitated for a few seconds.

He took a deep breath. Then he lowered his legs over the side.

CHAPTER 3

Max reached the bottom of the ladder. A row of bright ceiling lights came on. He found himself standing in a whitewashed room about the size of his classroom. The walls were full of hi-tech equipment. Black display panels and racks with red levers and green buttons surrounded him. A giant plasma screen hung on the wall.

"What is this place?" asked Max. He looked around. "And how long has it been here?"

"It was built before you were born," replied his dad.

MAX FLASH

"What? It's been down here my whole life. How come you never told me about it?"

"We couldn't," said his dad gently. "We had to wait for the right time."

His words hung in the air.

"There's someone we want you to meet," said his mom. She stepped over to a row of tiny green buttons. She pressed one.

In an instant, the plasma screen sprang to life. A woman's face appeared. She had

piercing blue eyes, high cheekbones, and thin, unsmiling lips. Her blonde hair was pulled back into a tight ponytail.

"Good evening, Max," said the woman. "My name is Zavonne. I work for an organization called the DFEA."

Max's eyes moved from the screen and over to his parents. They smiled. But this didn't stop him from feeling like his brain was about to explode. What was going on down here?

"Lots of things will soon become clear," said Zavonne. "But let me start by telling you a little bit about the DFEA."

Max stared at her open-mouthed. He waited for her to go on.

"The DFEA stands for the Department for Extraordinary Activity. You won't have heard of it. You won't have read about it. You won't have seen it on TV. It is a very secret organization. The only people who know about it are the people who run the department and our undercover agents in the field. What I am about to tell you is highly classified information. You are not to repeat a single word of it to anyone outside of this room. Do you understand?"

Max thought about this for a few seconds. How could he agree to keep silent? He had no idea what this strange woman was going to tell him. On the other hand, it felt like she was about to share something pretty amazing with

him. After all, coming through a secret door in your cellar and ending up in some sort of techno pod didn't happen every day. Did he really want to miss out?

He nodded slowly.

"Good," replied Zavonne briskly. "The DFEA deals with 'extraordinary' matters. These are situations or events that can't be explained. Things that the government, security services, the police, and the army could never handle."

Max looked confused. "What kind of extraordinary things?"

"Recent missions include healing a street sweeper who was possessed by the soul of the great Egyptian ruler Tutankhamen. And disabling an ambulance that kept time-traveling back to the French Revolution in Paris."

Max burst out laughing. He waited for Zavonne and his parents to join in.

But they remained silent.

Surely she wasn't serious?

He stared into Zavonne's cool eyes.

She was serious.

"This is a prank, right?" Max asked. His voice wobbled with uncertainty. "We're secretly being filmed for some practical joke show, aren't we? It has to be."

"We know this must be very hard for you to understand," said his mom softly. "But everything Zavonne says is true. The DFEA is a real organization doing absolutely important work. Dad and I have carried out two major missions. That's why this communications center is down here."

Max's mouth dropped open. He suddenly eyed his parents in a brand new light.

MAX FLASH
MISSION 1

CHAPTER 4

Missions? What was she talking about?
This was his mom and dad. They were stage
magicians. They shopped at the supermarket.
They went on camping trips! They weren't
some kind of weird undercover agents. They
didn't deal with Egyptian mummies or time-
traveling ambulances.

"What were the missions?" he asked.

"Ten years ago, we stopped mutant Saharan
sandmen from kidnapping the royal family,"
replied his mom.

"And three years ago, we destroyed a gang of Tellan Warriors. They had come from the twenty-fifth century to colonize Earth," said his dad.

"Yeah, right!" said Max. His shock turned to frustration. "Next, you'll be telling me we're all going to live on Mars and spend the rest of our lives eating space dust."

Zavonne's expression hardened. "I understand why this is difficult for you to believe, Max. But I assure you, this is not some sort of game. It is deadly serious."

Max looked at his parents. "Well, where was I when you fought those Tell Tale warriors or whatever they were called?"

"We hired a babysitter," replied his mom. "It was only a short battle."

Everyone was silent for a few moments. Max gradually realized that this might not be some crazy practical joke.

In fact, with each new revelation, it was starting to sound more and more real.

"OK," said Max slowly, eyeing his parents.

CHAPTER 5

"Let's say everything I've just heard is true. Why were *you* chosen for these missions?"

"Because of their magic skills," cut in Zavonne. "As you know, your parents are extremely experienced magicians. That's why they were chosen."

"But why are you telling me all this now?" Max demanded.

"Let me cut to the chase," said Zavonne. "The DFEA needs your help."

"M...m...me?" spluttered Max. "Why me?"

"You are a superb escape artist," answered Zavonne. "Plus, you are a child."

"What's being a child got to do with anything?"

"That will become apparent in a moment," replied Zavonne. "Let's start with the computer company Nexus Scope. You're familiar with their games, right?"

Familiar with them! Nexus Scope was the hottest gaming company in the world. Max had played loads of their games. *Centurion Warlords* and *Bogey Flickers* were his favorites.

"Our IT unit has come across something very strange at Nexus Scope," said Zavonne. "Ricky Stevens is one of their lead programmers. He has just completed the prototype of a new game called *Slime Beasts of Death.*"

Max raised an eyebrow.

Slime Beasts of Death?

That sounded good. Lots of gooey monsters to crush and splatter!

"But there's a problem," said Zavonne. "Ricky has lost one of the characters from his game. The character's name is Deezil. He is a freaky half-man, half-lizard. He's colored red and gold."

Max frowned and mentally replayed Zavonne's statement. "What do you mean *lost*?"

"Even though Ricky has created every single micrometer of the game," Zavonne replied,

"he can't locate Deezil anywhere on his hard drive."

Max stared at her in silence.

"But that's only part of the problem," Zavonne added. "There were two events in central London this morning that came to our attention. One was in a corner shop. The other was at a railway station. In each case, witnesses reported seeing a terrifying red-and-gold beast attacking bystanders. It smashed up furniture. It threatened to kill any gamer who stood in his way. Witnesses were badly shaken. The police attended both of these incidents. Fortunately, we were able to get our people to these scenes shortly afterward. Our agents were able to wipe out all of the witnesses' memories of these events. And they cleared the police officers using De-Memory Mist."

Max felt his chest tighten. "You're not trying to say that...?"

"Yes, Max," replied Zavonne. "I'm saying that Ricky Stevens has created a portal between

the Virtual world and our world. Or the "gamer
world," as Deezil called it. Somehow, Deezil has
located the portal and visited us. We're pretty
sure he's returned to the Virtual world. But
we have no idea if or when he's going to come
back. Or what he might do if he does."

"So why don't you just get Ricky Stevens to
close the portal?" said Max.

Zavonne shook her head. "Ricky has no idea
that he's created this portal. We want to keep
it that way. He's spooked enough about losing
Deezil from *Slime Beasts of Death*. Luckily,
he hasn't told anyone yet. If we let him know
about the portal, he'd completely freak out.
Within five minutes, the whole planet would
know about it. Can you imagine the chaos that
would cause?"

"Can't the DFEA close it?" asked Max.

Zavonne sighed. "We have the finest
programmers on Earth working for us," she
replied. "They've hacked into Ricky's computer.

They've carried out exhaustive searches of his hard drive. They are sure the portal was created by a one-in-a-billion accident. But so far they have not been able to close it."

She paused for a second and stared at Max.

"I don't get it," said Max. "What do you want me to do?"

"We need someone to visit the Virtual world and shut down the portal. We must stop Deezil from reentering our world and causing far worse trouble. And that someone, Max, is you."

Max snorted. "That's mad! Even if I believed half of what you're saying, there's no way a human could ever visit the virtual world! It's totally impossible!"

"Hear me out," said Zavonne. "Let me explain my plan. In one hour, Nexus Scope is holding a special tour of their headquarters for some winners of an Internet competition. We got you a ticket."

Max's pulse quickened.

A tour inside Nexus Scope? Wicked!

"You will attend this event and locate Ricky Stevens's work station. Seven USB ports on his hard drive are being used. But the eighth one is empty. I need you to insert something called an EP-NR USB hub into the back of that hard drive. We've spent years developing this hub. This will be the first time it's been used. If all goes as planned, the second you connect the hub you will be powered straight inside Ricky Stevens's hard drive."

Max couldn't stifle his nervous giggle. "No way!"

"I understand your shock," Zavonne said. "But this is an absolutely crucial mission. There is a huge amount at stake. If Deezil gets out again, we have no idea how much damage he could cause. It could get out of control quickly. We cannot let that happen, Max. Deezil must be stopped."

Max drew in some air and puffed out his cheeks.

"What happens if I say no?" he asked.

"No one has ever said no to me," replied Zavonne coldly.

"I can't believe this is happening!" muttered Max. He tried to process all that he had seen and heard in the last few minutes.

He turned to face his parents. "If I agree to it, can I skip my homework this weekend?"

His mom and dad glanced at each other. They both nodded.

Max gulped nervously and turned back to Zavonne. "OK," he said. "I'll do it."

"Good," said Zavonne. "Now open that drawer in front of you."

A silver drawer flashed on the wall to Max's right. He walked over and pulled it open.

This is not a dream, he told himself. *This is actually happening.*

MAX FLASH MISSION 1

CHAPTER 6

Inside the drawer was a map, a pass for the Nexus Scope Open Day, and a computer hub marked EP-NR. There was also a zip-up shirt, some cargo pants, and a sleek new pair of running shoes.

"You have agreed to take on this mission," announced Zavonne. "You are now officially a DFEA Agent. You may talk to your parents about the mission but to no one else."

Max nodded. He studied the clothes, the map, and the hub.

"You know what the hub is for. And the Open Day pass is self-explanatory," Zavonne said. "The map contains the layout of the Nexus Scope headquarters. The Programmers' Den is highlighted in red. Ricky Stevens' workstation is fifth on the left."

"What's with the clothes?" asked Max. "Why can't I wear my own gear?"

"These may seem like ordinary clothes, but they are far from it," Zavonne replied. "Each item is heatproof, fireproof, bulletproof, waterproof, and any other proof you'd care to mention. They're also self-cleaning. They never need to be washed."

Max's eyes lit up. A break from having to drag things to the laundry basket!

"You will notice that the pants have three pockets," Zavonne went on. "In each pocket you will find a gadget. These have been developed in top secret DFEA labs."

Gadgets?

Max loved gadgets. He and his parents used all sorts of gadgets in their show. He reached into the pockets. He pulled out a pack of cards, a can of deodorant, and a small flashlight. He felt a wave of disappointment wash over him. He'd been hoping for a laser gun, something cool like that.

"The spray is a Multi-Hologram Spray," explained Zavonne. "When you push the button, twenty realistic, life-size versions of you will appear. It will confuse even the smartest opponents. It will buy you some time to escape, if you need it."

Max turned the spray over in his hands. *OK, that sounds pretty good.*

"The cards," continued Zavonne, "are Stair Flight Cards. Once you release them, they will create a flight of steps as high in the air as you throw them. And the small flashlight is a Universal Hole Burner. It will burn a hole in any surface. The hole will close after five seconds."

Max smiled. *Burn holes in any surface? Cool!*

"Can I try them out now?" he asked excitedly.

Zavonne shook her head. "Each gadget can only be used once. You may only use them when your life is in danger, Max. They are not toys."

Max returned the gadgets to the pockets of the cargos.

"Can Max get hurt inside the hard drive?" asked his mom. "Even though Virtuals are straight back on their feet when a player starts a new game, there's no proof that they don't feel any pain. They may not get killed. But they might get hurt or

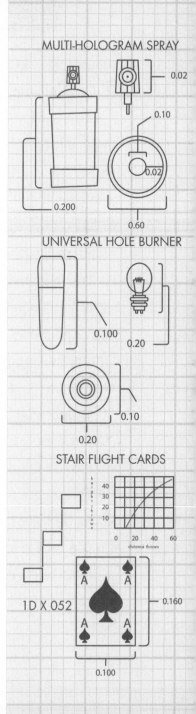

MULTI-HOLOGRAM SPRAY

0.02
0.10
0.02
0.200
0.60

UNIVERSAL HOLE BURNER

0.100
0.20

0.10
0.20

STAIR FLIGHT CARDS

40
30
20
10
0   20   40   60
distance thrown

A A
A A

1D X 052

0.160

0.100

injured. Surely, if Deezil can get out through the portal, anything is possible."

Zavonne looked at the three of them impassively. Max's dad cut in. "It's a good point," he said, nodding. "Max will be the first gamer ever to enter the virtual world. We have no idea what will happen to him if he's attacked by a monster in one of the games."

"You are quite correct. We don't know if virtual characters can feel any pain. And I can't guarantee that Max won't get hurt."

Max saw his parents look at each other with concern.

"This briefing is nearly over," said Zavonne. "I won't see you again until the after the mission."

"Er, I've got a question," piped up Max. "How do I get back? Can I use the EP-NR hub for the return journey?"

"Everything will become clear to you when you are on the other side, Max."

"Can't you be a little bit more specific?" asked Max's mom. "He's our only child. We do want him back."

Zavonne replied curtly: "I have every confidence that Max will be able to handle any challenges that face him. Now, if there are no further questions, this briefing is over."

Zavonne suddenly vanished, and the screen went blank.

MAX FLASH

MISSION 1

CHAPTER 7

Max's dad pulled the car up in front of
the large iron gates of the Nexus Scope
headquarters. His mom had given him an
extra-tight hug when they'd said good-bye at
home.

Max was wearing the DFEA clothes. They
fit him perfectly. He felt once more for the
gadgets in his pockets. He held the map tightly
in his fist. In his other hand he held the pass
that Zavonne had given him.

"Get the job done as quickly as possible,"

said his dad. "And don't take any unnecessary risks."

"I'll do my best, Dad," Max replied. He felt a rush of fear and excitement.

He opened the door and stepped out of the car.

Five minutes later, Max was inside the New Product Trial room with thirty other kids. There was a row of technicians wearing silver headphones checking out some games in progress.

The man conducting the tour of Nexus Scope had a voice that droned like an old air conditioner. He gave them a long speech about the history of the company. Then he turned and headed for some doors on the far side of the room.

Max hung back, waiting for the right opportunity to split from the group. As the guide reached the doors, Max slipped through a side door. He carefully checked the map

Zavonne had given him. He hurried up a
flight of metal steps. He passed through a
set of automatic gates and strode along a
corridor. He finally reached a blue door marked
Programmers' Den.

He slowly pushed the door open. He entered
a space bursting with workstations and
computers.

Max checked the map one more time. He
stopped at the fifth workstation on the left.
Max pulled the EP-NR hub out of his top
pocket. He knelt down on his hands and knees
and crawled under the desk. He turned the
hard drive around and looked at the bank of
wires and connection points.

Thoughts and questions fizzed through his
brain. *This is so unreal! It's mad! What if the
hub doesn't connect properly? What if it
doesn't work? What if there's a massive
explosion and I'm blown to bits?*

His heart thumped.

Zavonne seems to know what she's talking about. But it's me who is actually taking the risk!

Max wiped a trickle of sweat off his forehead. He studied the back of the hard drive. Just as Zavonne had briefed him, there was a row of eight USB ports.

Seven had hubs connected.

One was empty.

Max took a very deep breath and pushed the hub into the empty port.

The second the hub connected to the socket, Max was surrounded by a bright flash of white light. His body plummeted downward at terrifying speed.

CHAPTER 8

Max landed on his feet with a heavy thud. He was standing in a gleaming, metallic corridor that stretched as far as he could see. On each side of the corridor was a series of closed metal hatches.

He turned to his left and began to walk slowly down the corridor. Each metal hatch had a sign above it: *Bash the Cash, Bogey Flickers, Mutant Snake Attack, Death City Survivors.* These were all Nexus Scope games Max had played.

It's worked!

It's really worked!

I'm actually inside the hard drive of Ricky Stevens's computer! How cool is that? It isn't just some practical joke. It's the real deal! What a killer that I can't brag to any of my friends about this!

But where was the hatch leading to *Slime Beasts of Death?* It might take ages to track it down.

Ricky Stevens is a computer programmer. He'll have zillions of games on his hard drive! And what if I can't find the right hatch? I don't want to get stuck in this corridor.

At that exact moment, Max spotted a hatch further down on the left.

It was half open.

But it was closing fast.

He made a split-second decision.

He sprinted forward and dived under the hatch. He rolled to a halt and stood up.

The hatch slammed shut behind him.

Max looked around. He was standing on a large strip of tarmac. Crowds were cheering. A deep roar came from somewhere behind him. The sound was getting louder by the second.

"GET OFF THE TRACK!" someone shouted.

Max looked up. His eyes nearly fell out of their sockets.

He was standing in the middle of a racetrack. In front of him was a giant spectator stand bursting with fans. The crowd cheered and clapped excitedly.

He knew this game. It was *FX Turbo Racer*. He'd played it loads of times! It was all about top speed and screeching tires. In the distance he could hear the roar of the powerful cars. Max knew they could all reach over 250 miles per hour. No wonder Zavonne had selected him for this mission. His parents wouldn't have a clue about any of these games!

"I said MOVE!"

The voice was coming from a man in an orange tracksuit. He stood behind a meshed fence and waved his arms wildly.

Max quickly looked at the grey tarmac with its white markings. He could see sharp curves in both directions, each about a hundred meters away.

Zavonne's words flashed through his mind: *I can't guarantee that Max won't get hurt.*

He didn't want to stay on the track to test that out. He spun around nervously. There was no space at the side of the racetrack in *FX Turbo Racer.* So where was he going to go?

The engine noise was deafening. He watched with horror as the cars hurtled around the top bend. They were bearing down on him furiously.

His heart hammered against his ribcage. He panicked. But then he remembered the gadgets. In a split second, he reached into his pocket and yanked out the pack of Stair Flight Cards. The cars were nearly upon him now. He flicked open the lid. He threw the cards into the air.

They spilled out and instantly formed a flight of stairs just above the track.

Max leaped onto the first step. The first car thundered by just centimeters below him.

Quickly, he took another couple of steps. The remaining vehicles sped beneath his body. Talk about a close shave! He marveled at the genius of the cards. Then he—and they—suddenly fell down onto the track.

Max was very familiar with the track layout. And he knew the cars would be around again in less than a minute. He had to act quickly.

About twenty meters up the track was a partly concealed pit stop. Parked in this space was an empty red car. Max heard the screech of the speeding cars pounding towards the top bend again. He ran toward the red car as fast he could.

MAX FLASH
MISSION 1
CHAPTER 9

Max reached the car as the other racers took the top bend. He grabbed the door handle. He yanked it open. To his huge relief, he saw a key in the ignition. He slid into the driver's seat. He pulled the door shut and snapped on the seatbelt.

He glanced in the rearview mirror.

The other cars were nearly on top of him!

Frantically, he turned the key. The car growled to life. He grabbed the steering wheel and floored the accelerator.

The car lurched. The speedometer climbed from 0 to 60 in two seconds.

This was crazy! He was inside an *FX Turbo Racer* car!

His speed passed 100 miles an hour, then 200. He checked his mirror again. The cars were screaming toward him. They were less than twenty meters away.

He remembered that a nasty bend was coming up. He gritted his teeth. He roared around the bend at 250 miles per hour. His car spun violently onto the straight. It skidded first left and then right. He had to use all of his strength to steer the vehicle back onto the track.

But he'd lost a vital couple of seconds. A dark green car was now beside him on the outside of the track. Without any warning, the driver of the green car suddenly cranked the steering wheel hard and smashed into the side of Max's car.

Max cried out in shock. His car hurtled towards a huge billboard. His elbow banged against the door. Max winced. That was the answer to one of his most crucial questions. He *could* feel pain in the Virtual world.

Max's mind was a blur. What was going on? *FX Turbo Racer* wasn't some violent demolition derby. You didn't take out other cars. It was an exciting but straightforward racing simulator.

His car bounced off a massive steel pylon at the bottom of the billboard. He heard the sickening scrape of metal against metal. Sparks shot into the air.

He looked sideways. The driver of the green car was laughing like a maniac. He was already turning his wheel hard for another collision.

Max's brain frantically tried to make sense of what was happening. He spotted a yellow car scorching up on his inside. The driver of this car was also laughing with glee.

Max groaned.

Now he was going to be sandwiched between these two complete madmen.

At the exact same second, the green and yellow drivers turned their steering wheels. Their cars veered toward Max.

But Max was ready for them.

Thank goodness he'd played *FX Turbo Racer* so many times. He flicked the booster switch

on the dashboard. Instantly, his red car flew forward. The green and yellow drivers realized what he'd done. But they were too late. As Max sped out of their way, the other two cars crunched into each other. Shards of glass and metal went flying across the track. A couple of seconds later, the remaining vehicles smashed into the green and yellow ones. All of the cars were now tangled up. They zigzagged down the track together like a twisted metal monster.

Max watched the horrific pileup in his rearview mirror. He didn't see the red-and-gold figure running across the track until the last second. He braked hard and skidded out of the way.

He pushed open the door and leaped out.

Had he nearly crashed into *Deezil?* He spotted the blurred figure running through an orange door beneath one of the spectator stands. Max sprinted after it a split second

before the wrecked cars smashed into a giant
stone wall. But instead of screams coming from
the drivers of the cars, Max heard laughter and
cheering. Could Deezil be somehow responsible
for this new, scary anarchy?

He shuddered. He turned back to the stands
and sped through the orange door.

MAX FLASH MISSION 1

CHAPTER 10

The door led into a dimly lit, narrow
passageway. The door swung shut behind
him. The cheers of the crowd faded to silence.
Max crept along the passage. He searched all
around him to get a closer look at the blurred
shape he'd followed. But as he approached the
end, there was an ear splitting crash. He lost
his footing. He was tossed violently forward.
His left shoulder took the main force of the
impact. He rolled over as he hit the floor.

He opened his eyes and looked up. He saw
an arrow heading straight for his head.

MAX FLASH MISSION 1

CHAPTER 11

Max ducked. The arrow whistled a millimeter above his head. He quickly scanned his surroundings. He was in a deep valley. It was dotted with clumps of trees and surrounded by ragged brown mountains. The entire valley was crawling with thousands of Roman centurions locked in battle.

Max knew at once that he was in *Centurion Warlords*.

Centurion Warlords was a game of strategy and quick thinking. It pitted Prince Byzantor's army against his deadly enemy, Emperor Frelic.

But the scene in front of him was very different from the version he was used to. Like the drivers in *FX Turbo Racer,* the centurions weren't confined to their normal fighting abilities. They were completely out of control. They kicked, punched, swiveled, and pirouetted.

Another arrow whizzed through the air. Max jumped out of its way. He looked at his clothes and realized he couldn't be mistaken for a Virtual. His zip-up top, cargo pants, and running shoes weren't exactly Roman. He had to get his hands on some centurion gear. And quick!

Of course! He knew exactly where to go.

Max spun around. He looked up a craggy hill and began running. He passed several

mighty sword fights and some armor-to-armor tussling. A fireball crashed just over his head. It smashed into a large wooden gate, throwing up a huge cloud of splinters and flames.

Max gulped and sped on. A minute later he plowed into a large row of dense bushes. It was lucky that he knew the layout of the game. These bushes hid the entrance to a secret cave that served as Prince Byzantor's armory.

Max stepped into the mouth of the cave. He rounded a sharp bend.

A steely-faced man in a yellow robe sat behind a long oak desk. He was studying a piece of parchment. Behind him were rows and rows of swords, shields, and maces hanging on hooks on the cave's walls. The man looked up when he heard Max approaching.

"I am Thadius," snorted the man. "State your name!"

"Er, I'm Maximus," Max replied.

"What are those strange garments you wear?"

"They're ... they're foreign," Max answered. "A smuggler sold them to me. But I need some armor."

Thadius eyed him with contempt. "You're very small for a centurion," he snapped.

"True," Max agreed. "But I'm still handy with a sword."

"Listen, Maximus," the angry official hissed.

"The lizard god Deezil has visited this valley. He has shown us that we can control our own movements in battle. We are not at the mercy of the Gamers. For that, we are eternally grateful. But we of Prince Byzantor's army are still dedicated to fighting Emperor Frelic. The man is a tyrant. He must be defeated. I suppose we need as many soldiers as we can recruit. I will find you some smaller pieces of armor."

Thadius stood up. He pulled several sections of armor off the cave wall. He reached for a huge silver shield and a long sword in a scabbard.

Max slipped the top section of body armor over his head. Then he put on the bottom section. He pulled on the visor with the yellow Byzantor crest. Emperor Frelic's men wore a purple crest on their visors.

Max squinted through the narrow arc of space at the front of the helmet.

I'll be lucky if I can see my feet, let alone the hordes of Frelic's evil warlords! he thought.

"Can I ask you a question?" Max asked through the hole in his visor.

"What is it?" snapped Thadius.

"Now that the centurions can control their own movements, do they feel any pain?"

Thadius eyed him suspiciously. "Of course they don't feel real pain. Before the great lizard

god appeared, we were programmed by the Gamers to bleed or die when attacked. But it was all for show. Then we were forced to fall

to the ground and play hurt or dead until the gamer started up another game."

"And since Deezil arrived?" asked Max.

"We still have the ability not to be injured or killed. Only now we don't have to lie down and wait for a gamer to restart the battle."

"But if you can't kill or injure one another, how is anyone ever going to win the battle?" asked Max.

"We can lock up our enemies. We can cage them. We can bind them with thick ropes!" snorted Thadius. "And that is what we intend to do with all of Frelic's men. The battle will continue! Prince Byzantor will be victorious!"

"Go Byzantor!" shouted Max, a bit too enthusiastically.

"Enough talk, mini-centurion!" thundered Thadius. "It is high time you went into battle!"

Max clanked out of the cave and back through the bushes.

Talk about hard to walk! It's a miracle I can even stay upright!

He looked down into the valley. There was no sign of a red-and-gold lizard man.

If only I can track him down, I'm sure he'd lead me to that portal!

Max was halfway up a stony path when a massive centurion suddenly blocked his way. On his visor was a purple crest. He was one of Frelic's soldiers. And he was raising his sword high into the air.

CHAPTER 12

In panic, Max held up his shield. The
centurion's blade thudded against it. The
impact left a large dent in the shield.

Max's relief lasted less than a nanosecond.
Frelic's man was lifting his sword again. Max
looked out of his visor in horror. As the sword
reached its peak, Max swung his heavy blade
against the centurion's knees using every
ounce of strength. The blow was powerful
enough. It sent the centurion reeling backward.
He toppled over and crashed to the ground.

Max felt a surge of adrenaline. He hurried away from the fallen centurion. He looked around. He tried to catch a glimpse of Deezil. He'd just reached a narrow stone path when he spied one of Frelic's men on horseback. He was riding straight toward him. The centurion was swinging a sword.

Max looked around desperately. He heard
Zavonne's words ringing in his ears.

*You may only use them when your life is in
danger.*

Well, his life was certainly in danger. But
the infuriating armor meant he couldn't
get anywhere near his gadgets. The horse
thundered forward. The mounted centurion
raised his sword.

*Please let me die without too much
pain.*

But when Frelic's centurion was almost
upon him, a booming noise erupted in the
valley.

"THIS IS YOUR LEADER, DEEZIL!"

Instantly, the rider pulled up his horse.
Dropping his sword, he dismounted and knelt
on the ground. Max looked around. All over the
valley, centurions were falling to their knees.
Max followed as quickly as his armor would let
him.

"A TRUCE HAS BEEN CALLED," Deezil bellowed.

There were gasps all around.

"ALL CENTURIONS MUST REPORT TO THE DUST BOWL IMMEDIATELY!"

In an instant, every centurion in the valley was marching toward the dust bowl. Max clanked forward with the rest. He wondered why Deezil had commanded them to stop fighting. The battlefield had been total chaos a moment ago. Why did Deezil have the power to stop the bloodshed?

Frelic's men were gathering on the left side of the dust bowl. Byzantor's troops were on the right. As soon as each centurion arrived, he fell to his knees.

And at that instant, Max saw Deezil for the first time.

The lizard man stood on top of a gigantic rock at the far side of the bowl. Up close, he was truly grotesque. His top half was bright red. It had narrow sections of flesh missing, revealing hideously sharp bones that jutted out at every angle. His bottom half was covered in oily scales. Each scale dripped some sort of dark slime.

Max shuddered. He knelt down with the rest of the centurions.

"I AM HERE TO TELL YOU," roared Deezil,

"THAT BEING ABLE TO CONTROL YOUR MOVEMENTS IS ONLY THE START OF MY GRAND PLAN!"

Centurions whispered among themselves.

"WE MUST NOW RISE UP AND BATTLE FOR TOTAL FREEDOM!"

Max looked over his shoulder. Thousands more centurions poured into the dust bowl every second and fell to their knees.

"YOU MUST PUT ASIDE THE HATRED THAT EXISTS BETWEEN PRINCE BYZANTOR AND EMPEROR FRELIC—FOREVER!"

The centurions looked confused.

"GAMERS CREATED US," roared Deezil. "THEY *ENSLAVED* US WITH OUR LIMITED MOVES!"

"But couldn't we coexist with the Gamers?" asked one of Byzantor's men. "Or ask them to grant us more moves?"

Deezil stared at the man with fury and contempt. "THERE WILL BE NO COEXISTENCE!

THE GAMERS TRAPPED US HERE. WE OWE THEM NOTHING!"

"But it's always been this way!" shouted one of Frelic's men.

"WELL, IT ENDS NOW!" shrieked Deezil. He was hopping about with excitement. "THE GAMERS ARE OUR FOES. WE WILL FIGHT THEM ALL!"

"How can we fight them?" called out several centurions.

"A DOOR HAS OPENED BETWEEN OUR WORLD AND THEIRS," hissed Deezil. "I HAVE ALREADY VISITED THE OTHER SIDE."

Gasps of shock rang throughout the valley.

"What's it like?" shouted lots of voices.

"IT'S INCREDIBLE!" shrieked Deezil maniacally. "THEY HAVE KEPT ALL OF THE GOOD THINGS FOR THEMSELVES. THEY ARE HIDEOUS, SELFISH BEINGS WHO MUST BE DESTROYED. WE NEED TO PREPARE

OURSELVES FOR THE ATTACK. I WANT
EVERY SWORD SHARPENED. EVERY SHIELD
CHECKED. EVERY SUIT OF ARMOR HAMMERED
INTO SHAPE. FROM THIS MOMENT ON, YOU
WILL NOT RAISE YOUR WEAPONS AGAINST
EACH OTHER. YOU ARE NOW ON THE SAME
SIDE!"

There was dead silence. Then an outbreak
of cheering and shouting erupted. Centurions
from opposite sides were suddenly shaking
hands and hugging each other through the
heavy suits of armor.

Max felt his throat tighten.

This was way beyond scary. Deezil wasn't
happy to just visit the Gamers' world and carry
on with his life in the Virtual world. No, his plan
was obvious now. Deezil wanted to lead all of
the characters from the Virtual world through
the portal. He wanted to take on the Gamers.

The very future of human existence was at
stake!

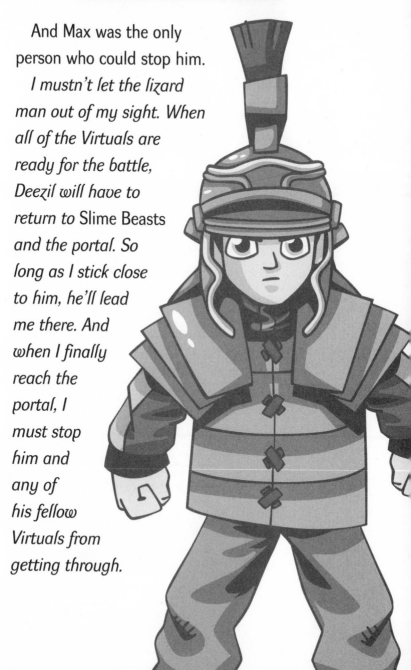

And Max was the only person who could stop him.

I mustn't let the lizard man out of my sight. When all of the Virtuals are ready for the battle, Deezil will have to return to Slime Beasts and the portal. So long as I stick close to him, he'll lead me there. And when I finally reach the portal, I must stop him and any of his fellow Virtuals from getting through.

Max's attention was brought back to Deezil.

"ENOUGH!" shouted the lizard man.

There was immediate silence in the dust bowl.

He paused for a few seconds.

"WE WILL FIGHT THE GAMERS. AND WE WILL DEFEAT THEM!"

Another colossal bout of cheering and clapping rang out.

Don't take your eyes off Deezil, Max's brain urged him.

But a second later, a great chinking of metal sounded. The centurions rose to their feet. They headed back to their bases to prepare for battle against the Gamers. Max found himself swept up in the vast crowd as it herded its way back out of the dust bowl. Max wriggled furiously as he was dragged along.

"Let me go," he shouted. "I have to get back there."

But the force of the crowd was immense.

Max glanced around. He saw Deezil leaping down from the rock and holding an intense conversation with several centurions.

"Please!" screamed Max. "You have to let me go!"

But his cries were ignored. The mass of bodies pulled him on.

And with every step, he was being taken further and further away from the evil lizard man.

CHAPTER 13

Ten minutes later, Max finally managed to break away from the mass of bodies. He made his way back to the gigantic rock in the dust bowl. To his despair, all traces of Deezil were gone.

He hurried out of the bowl and began to search the valley. Everywhere, centurions were working on battle preparations. It was so weird seeing Frelic's men and Byzantor's men sitting together. They were sharpening their swords, banging dented pieces of armor back into shape, and sharing battle stories.

He stopped several times to ask groups of centurions if they'd seen Deezil. Or if they knew where he could find *Slime Beasts of Death* and the portal. But none of them had a clue. After an hour of searching, Max found himself back at the cave. Thadius was still seated behind his desk. But he'd brightened up a bit. Now he was only scowling rather than shouting.

"You again?" said Thadius.

"Me again," smiled Max weakly.

"Make yourself useful," Thadius said. "Go and give Savasha a hand. She's a Barbarian slave. I warn you, she has a loose tongue."

Max glanced over. He spotted a young woman scraping a piece of stone against a metal blade. She muttered angrily. Savasha looked about eighteen. She had long blonde hair and emerald-green eyes.

"Can I help you?" asked Max, walking over to her.

She looked up. Upon seeing Max, she spat

on the floor.

"You're pathetic," she hissed. "Every one of you! Curse Emperor Frelic! And curse Prince Byzantor!"

"Hi, I'm Max. Er, I mean, Maximus." He smiled, trying to win her over with his charm.

She spat on the ground again. She held her stone still for a moment. "All it took was for that creature Deezil to shout at you, and you all stopped fighting!" she snarled. "Call yourselves men?"

"But didn't you hear what he said about rising up against the

Gamers?" Max asked.

"Pah!" snorted Savasha. "What happens if the Virtuals lose that battle, huh? The Gamers could make all of us their slaves. Conditions on the other side could be worse than here!"

"So what are you going to do when the battle begins?" Max asked.

Savasha threw her head back and laughed. "You think I'd tell you? Some half-sized excuse for a Byzantor centurion!"

"Hang on," replied Max, a little offended. "I may be small. But I can tell you that things aren't always what they seem."

He hurried around the bend to the front of the cave. He took off his centurion gear. Thadius was too engrossed with a piece of parchment to notice. When Max came back, Savasha eyed him with shock.

"What have you done with your armor?" she asked.

"Help me!" he said. "I'll make sure you

escape from the clutches of these centurion warlords."

Savasha stared at him in surprise. "How can you make such a promise! You're a Virtual just like the rest of us."

"No, Savasha," Max replied coolly. "I'm a Gamer."

"Fascinating!" crowed a third voice.

Max and Savasha spun around.

There was Deezil, standing with a large group of fierce-looking centurions.

"We have a Gamer spy in our midst," growled Deezil. He stared at Max with a hideous grin. "This Gamer can only be in our world for one reason! He is here to ruin my plan! He intends to stop us from crossing over to his world!"

"What do you want us to do with him?" asked another of the centurions.

Deezil stuck out his tongue. He rolled it across his lips. It was forked and green and

coated with disgusting yellow slime.

"Kill him," he hissed.

CHAPTER 14

At that second, Max remembered the perfect gadget to help him escape.

Multi-Hologram Spray!

He grabbed the can from his pocket. He squeezed a powerful blast into the air. Twenty life-size, 3-D images of him were projected all over the cave. Deezil and the centurions looked around, completely bewildered. The real Max smiled as he turned and ran down the tunnel into the cave.

The tunnel was very dark. The only light

came from a faint glow in the distance. The cave smelled damp and mossy. Water dripped on Max's head every few meters. The tunnel led down into the depths of the cave. As Max fled, his mind fizzed with questions. Would the tunnel lead to an escape route? Might it take him a step closer to *Slime Beasts of Death* and the portal? Or would it be a dead end? Would Deezil's men trap him and kill him? The Multi-Hologram Spray bought him some time. But he could hear heavy footsteps pounding after him.

"THIS WAY!"

It was Deezil's voice.

"HURRY UP! THAT REVOLTING LITTLE GAMER COULD STAND BETWEEN US AND FREEDOM!"

Max sped up. He almost tripped and fell as he ran over pebbles and boulders.

"THERE HE IS!" shrieked Deezil.

Max looked over his shoulder. He could see dark shapes hot on his trail. Metal swords bounced against the tunnel walls, sending sparks into the air. Max was approaching the light. He could see a hole in the tunnel roof. Just beneath this was a crossroads with three gloomy paths.

Which should I take? The left one, the middle one, or the right one?

He knew that a wrong decision could cost him his life.

Which one? WHICH ONE?

He decided on the left path. Suddenly, something caught his eye.

"FASTER!" ordered Deezil. He hurtled forward and reached the crossroads. The centurions were right behind him. "WHERE IS HE?" screamed Deezil.

The centurions looked around. But there was no sign of the boy.

"FIND HIM!"

Deezil banged his right fist into the palm of his left hand. "He must be here somewhere!"

His voice echoed off the damp walls.

"There's no sign of him," called out a centurion.

"Right," snarled Deezil. "I want you three to take the left path. You three take the right path. The rest of you, we'll take the middle path."

The crunching footsteps took off again. After a couple of minutes, the noise faded.

Max breathed a huge sigh of relief. He had squeezed into a very narrow crack just a second before Deezil and the centurions had reached the crossroads. He'd held his breath as they searched for him. He'd seen them run off to continue their search. Max slipped out of his hiding place. He brushed the dust and cobwebs off his shirt. He stood still for a minute, thinking about Deezil's plan.

OK. Deezil was preparing all of the Virtuals on Ricky Stevens's hard drive to get through the portal and battle the Gamers. How many Virtuals could there be? Just think about all of

the centurions in *Centurion Warlords*. There were easily tens of thousands of them. And that was only one game. If every character in every game joined the Virtual army, there would be millions.

And it wasn't like the Gamers would have better weapons than the Virtuals. It was the other way around! Computer programmers had unknowingly armed Virtuals with the most destructive methods of attack. The combined might of the Gamers' forces would be no match for the Ubez people of *Flight of Pain*. The Ubez had unlimited numbers of nuclear rocket launchers. And what about the giant Mutant Ants from *Cloud Catastrophe*? They would use low-flying drone planes to spread Deadly Butt Mist and suffocate everything in their path.

The Gamers would get smashed!

Max stepped into the left tunnel and hurried along. About seventy meters down on the right, he spied a wooden stable door split in two. From beyond the door he could hear the muted sounds of thumping country music.

Max hated country music almost as much as he hated doing homework. But surely it was better than waiting for Deezil and the centurions to catch him?

MAX FLASH
MISSION 1
CHAPTER 15

Max pushed on the top half of the door. It didn't budge. He had no luck with the bottom half either. He gave the door a barge with his shoulder. Still nothing. Standing back, he aimed a high kick at the center of the door. Both halves flew open! As he sprang forwards, the music flooded his ears.

It was "Yankee Doodle" with a thumping bass and crashing beat.

Max's eyes adjusted to the light. He was in a lush green meadow. Fluffy sheep were grazing

all around him at the bottom of a gentle hill.
He couldn't see Deezil or any centurions. That
was a good start. A skinny girl with braids,
dazzling blue eyes, and a frilly dress suddenly
appeared at his side. She linked her arm
through his.

"Hi there, cowboy!" she yelled. "I'm Daisy
Do-Good! Welcome to *Farmyard Frolics!*"

Before Max could reply, Daisy skipped off up
the hill. Because their arms were linked, Max
had no choice other than to skip with her.

Max was so grateful that his friends couldn't
see him now! They would howl with laughter

at his humiliation. It would send him straight to the top of the embarrassment charts. He'd never be able to live it down!

Max knew all about Daisy Do-Good and *Farmyard Frolics.* He'd seen one of his friends' little sisters playing it. As far as he'd been able to tell, the point of the game was to create the world's tidiest and most organized farm.

That wasn't a proper game! Where was the combat? Where were the weapons?

"It's real crazy today," Daisy shouted as they neared the top of a hill. "We're rounding folks up for the big battle against those nasty Gamer critters. Mr. Deezil has got us all organized."

"Wait," urged Max. "This is all a terrible mistake. You can't go to war!"

"Say what?" asked Daisy. She let go of his arm and gave him a funny look.

"It'll be a disaster," hissed Max. "Loads of Virtuals and Gamers will be killed. Please, Daisy! You've got to trust me! Do you know where Deezil is or how I can get into *Slime Beasts of Death?*"

"What the heck is goin' on?" shouted a gruff voice. There was an old man with white hair and a scraggly white beard. He strode towards them carrying a pitchfork.

"This boy says the battle might not be such a good idea, Pa," replied Daisy. "Reckons Mr. Deezil is up to no good."

The man eyed Max with contempt.

"Mr. Deezil's just sent word that there's a Gamer kid on the loose. He's trying to stop us from getting through that portal," hissed Pa. "This must be him!"

"Oh my!" gasped Daisy in shock.

Pa nudged Max on the shoulder with the pitchfork.

"I know what I'm talking about," said Max quickly. "Deezil, I mean, Mr. Deezil, is a madman. Or mad lizard. Or, whatever, he's just . . . mad. He's leading you into all sorts of

dangers and he—"

"BUTTON IT!" cut in Pa. "Since Mr. Deezil entered our lives, we've been able to control our own moves. We've made this farm tidier and more organized than ever before. And Mr. Deezil has told us all about the Gamers' world. Do you really think we're just gonna sit here and turn down this opportunity? We're on our way. And there's nothing you can do to stop us! You and your Gamer buddies are welcome to the farm and everything else."

Max stared at Pa.

"What did you just say?" he asked.

"He said the Gamers are welcome to the

farm and everything else," replied Daisy helpfully.

Max felt as if several million lightbulbs went off in his brain.

Why hadn't he seen it earlier?

Deezil doesn't just want to take the Gamers on. He wants to swap places. While the lizard man and his fellow Virtuals take over the Gamer world, the Gamers would be shoved into the Virtual world. They would be forced to live here forever.

He had to get away from Pa and *Farmyard Frolics*. He had to find Deezil!

Max started speeding up the hill. He flew forward and reached the top of the hill in less than fifteen seconds. He glanced back over his shoulder. He was horrified to see Pa and a large gang of beefy farmworkers running after him. They yelled at him and waved their pitchforks furiously. Max sped down the other side of the hill. Up ahead was the farmhouse. It

had a porch the whole way around it.

In desperation, Max flew inside and dove through the first door he came to. He found himself whooshing through the air. He realized he must have stumbled upon the entrance to another game. Suddenly he was crashing through leaves. He found himself hanging onto a tree branch thirty meters above the ground. Hundreds of thick trees surrounded him. The air was hot and sticky. And shaking the bottom of Max's tree and laughing like a maniac stood a large, drooling, slimy, lime-green creature.

CHAPTER 16

Max gulped with terror. He stared down at
the beast. On the plus side, it looked like he'd
finally arrived in *Slime Beasts of Death*. On
the minus side, the hideous creature was now
climbing the tree.

Max tried to stay calm. He knew that facing
this monster would be his hardest challenge.
He'd known lots about the other games he'd
visited. But he knew absolutely nothing about
Slime Beasts.

It was a prototype.

The only person who'd ever played it was Ricky Stevens.

Max cursed the computer programmer. If it hadn't been for him accidentally creating the stupid portal, Max would be safe at home. He would not be here, facing a slimy death.

The beast was within arm's length. It reached out its disgusting arm. Max kicked it off. But the creature grabbed him with its other arm.

Max kicked out again. But the creature pried him away from the tree trunk. The two of them crashed to the ground.

Luckily for Max, they landed on a thick, dry bush. They bounced forward onto a patch of dry earth. Max untangled himself from the monster's grip. He sprung away. He swerved around and came face-to-face with the beast.

On the ground, it looked even more horrific.

It was well over six feet tall. Its gigantic hairy body was covered in oozing yellow spots. Its three mouths were crowded with hundreds of red teeth. And it had six bloodshot eyes. Max looked around to see if there were any other disgusting creatures. But he and the monster were alone.

"So you must be the Gamer boy!" hissed the beast. It eyed Max. Huge globs of black drool slid out of its mouth. "Deezil warned us about you. He said if we found you, we should eat you."

"I'd taste disgusting," shouted Max. "There's hardly any meat on me. I'm all bones."

Three fat, furry tongues slid out of three repulsive mouths.

"I LOVE bones," hissed the creature.

"OK then," cried Max. "Maybe, maybe I can help you with with your teeth."

"MY TEETH?" it roared.

"Yeah," Max nodded vigorously. "I know this great orthodontist. She could fit you with some braces to really sort out those mouths of yours."

The beast let out a low, angry growl. It made another swoop for Max.

Max darted out of its way.

It twisted around and stomped toward him.

"OK!" Max screamed. "We'll leave the braces. She could just do a shine and polish!"

The monster loomed over Max. It lowered its head until it was only a few centimeters from Max's face. Its breath smelled like engine oil and rotting cabbages. Close up, its skin was slimy. It oozed pus.

"She also does tooth whitening," yelled Max desperately. He took two more large steps back.

Suddenly, his back came up against a solid tree trunk.

The monster reached out its left hand. It grabbed Max by the neck.

"At last," it cackled. "Time for my meal!"

The creature lifted Max toward its lips. Max sank his teeth into one of its cheeks.

"AAAAAAAARRRRRRRRRGGGGHHHHHHH!" shrieked the monster. It released Max from its grasp. It fell crashing to the ground. Two of its zits exploded in a shower of yellow pus. A large splat landed on Max's head.

Euuuuurgghh! Disgusting.

The creature was now lying on the jungle floor. It howled and held its cheek in pain.

Max didn't hang around. He ran down a narrow track. He leaped over a stream overflowing with bubbling slime. He ran between some trees. The air was sticky and hot all around him.

I'm in Slime Beasts. The portal is somewhere in this game. If I find it, I might be able to close it. I have to stop Deezil's vile plan.

He tumbled into a small clearing. He was panting and drenched in sweat.

But before he could get back into his stride, he heard a terrific slam. Metal chains were

being wrapped tightly around his body.

Max saw at once that he was inside a small cage. He'd been tricked!

"I think this little game of yours is over!" hissed Deezil.

CHAPTER 17

"It's only just begun," snarled Max through the bars of the cage.

"Oh no it hasn't!" roared Deezil.

"Oh yes it..."

Max stopped himself. The situation was far too serious for comedy banter.

He shook his body. But the chains wouldn't budge.

Deezil laughed at his struggles. But then a ferocious scowl appeared on his face.

"I am sick and tired of you running around

this hard drive trying to unsettle my troops. Trying to get in the way of my glorious plan."

"It's *not* glorious," yelled back Max. "It's madness! You have no idea about what will happen to you and the Virtuals on the other side."

"I HAVE BEEN THERE!" bellowed Deezil.

"Yeah! For one hour," Max pointed out. "If you think it will be a straightforward battle, you're totally deluded. You could get all of your Virtual friends destroyed."

"I will not listen to you. The time has come to lead my people through the portal."

"NO!" Max pleaded. "You mustn't do it. The fallout will be gigantic!"

But Deezil wasn't prepared to listen to another word. He pulled out a silver microphone from a small pack resting on his shoulder. He switched it on.

"COMRADES! YOU MUST ALL GATHER NOW

BY THE PORTAL. THE TIME FOR BATTLE HAS
FINALLY COME!"

And with that, Deezil grabbed the long
handle at the front of the cage. He wheeled it
forward. Max tried the chains again.

There was no give.

It was finally over. He'd have to spend the
rest of his life as a prisoner in a hard drive. He
had to do something!

Deezil pulled Max along in the tiny cage.
They passed through the moist jungle air and
the vast thicket of trees. When they finally
emerged, Max saw they were in a huge, dried-
mud field.

On the far side of the field, in between
two slimy pools of sticky green lava, was an
opening hovering in midair. It was the height
and width of a regular door in the Gamers'
world. At last—the portal!

CHAPTER 18

"In a few moments," Deezil declared, his chest swelling with pride, "I will go through that portal with my fellow Virtuals. Millions and millions of us. And you will be left here, a powerless spectator to such a triumphant occasion." He cackled with laughter. "Just think!" he cried. "In a short while, you will be reunited with all of your filthy Gamer pals!"

Deezil grabbed the cage handle and started pulling it across the field.

In the background Max could hear the

noise of marching feet and cries of celebration. He turned around as far as he could. He saw shapes emerging from the trees.

It was the rest of the Virtuals!

There were the drivers from *FX Turbo Racer*, the Gargons and hundreds of other aliens from *Space Rage,* and countless centurions. Savasha the Barbarian slave was being nudged forward by Thadius. She did not look very happy about this. Daisy Do-Good, Pa, and a gang of farmhands traveled in the yellow truck. Hundreds of gruesome slime beasts marched forward. A large gang of cobras from *Mutant Snake Attack*. The Greenheads from *Bogey Flickers.* Armed vigilantes from *Bash the Cash*. Chrome-clad bikers from *Death City Survival.* Thousands more surged ahead.

It was a truly scary sight.

Deezil was hopping with glee.

"KEEP MOVING!" he cried to the Virtual army. "KEEP MOVING!"

Max gulped nervously.

The field was filling with Virtuals. Thousands more poured out from the trees.

Max kicked his the bars of the cage in frustration. As he did so, he felt a movement in one of the chains. The tip of his left elbow was free. He looked to see if Deezil had noticed. But the lizard man was still jumping about with delight. He was calling out greetings and urging the Virtuals to hurry up.

Max thought back to his water tank practice in the living room. He thought about the countless hours he'd spent sharpening his skills.

He was Max Flash, wasn't he? Master escape artist! He could do this!

He thrust his elbow back with a violent push. A chain slipped off his shoulder. He wriggled his shoulder back and forth. Another chain came loose. He now had momentum. After several tugs, twists, and turns, he was

free. Max tried to squeeze an elbow between the cage's bars. But he didn't have enough room to angle it through.

The lizard man was less than twenty meters away from the portal. Suddenly he let out a ferocious scream.

The portal was starting to close.

CHAPTER 19

Max eyed it with absolute astonishment. Why was this happening? *How* was it happening?

Deezil turned violently toward Max.

"THIS IS YOUR DOING!" he screamed.

"I wish it was," shouted Max. "But it's not me."

At that very second, strange things began happening.

The Virtuals froze in their tracks. Then they start to move in straight lines and perfect arcs. Some were walking backward. Others were

crashing into each other. Some were raising their arms repeatedly in the air. Others were running back to the trees with speedy, robotic movements.

Max realized instantly what was happening.

The open portal had enabled the Virtuals to control their own movements. But as the portal was closing, these powers were taken away. The Virtuals were being dragged away from the portal, taken back to their home games.

But who had deactivated the portal? It wasn't me. And it obviously wasn't Deezil.

They were all moving in the ways that Max had always seen, the ways that Ricky Stevens and the other programmers had designed. They weren't going to make it through the portal. But the same couldn't be said for Deezil.

The lizard man dropped the handle of the cage. He was desperately fighting the force

that was tugging him away from the portal.
And even though it was a terrible struggle for
him, he was making small steps toward the
portal. He was only about ten meters away.

Max panicked.

OK. The Virtuals weren't going to get
through the portal. This was good.

But Deezil was determined. He was nearly
there. This was bad. This was very bad.

*What would Harry Houdini do in a situation
like this? Think!*

Max crashed backward. He managed to
get his right hand through one of the bars.
He followed this with his right shoulder. He
eased his head through. Next, he collapsed
his body to make it as thin as possible.
He began to push first his chest, then his
stomach through.

He glanced up.

Deezil was straining every sinew in his
body. He was less than five meters away from

the portal. A couple more steps and he'd be through.

Max gritted his teeth. With a tremendous push, he forced his waist through the bars. Then out came his legs. And finally his feet.

Deezil was now less than a meter away from the portal. In an instant he'd be through. It would be game over for Max.

I must stop him!

CHAPTER 20

Max sprinted forward and jumped in front of the portal. He blocked Deezil's way. The lizard man howled with rage. He tried to take a swipe at Max. Max held up his arms to deflect the blow. But none came. Deezil's movements spluttered to a halt. His sharp nails were inches from Max's face. Max eyed the portal. He figured that he had less than five minutes before it closed completely. He hurled Deezil into the cage. He dragged him back through the trees. Up ahead, he could see enormous

lines of Virtuals moving through a hatch next to a rocky waterfall.

Max spotted the slimy creature that had attacked him. It was settling down into a giant mud bath. The other Slime Beasts were wandering off to their regular hangouts.

"WHERE ARE YOU TAKING ME?" shrieked Deezil. "Put me down here in my own game. I promise you I'll stay in *Slime Beasts of Death* and never trouble you again."

"Interesting offer," said Max. "But I'm afraid the answer's NO."

As Max strode through the hatch, he found himself back in the long, gleaming corridor where he had first arrived in Ricky Stevens's hard drive.

As far as he could see, huge numbers of Virtuals moved up and down the corridor. They were disappearing through hatches and returning to their own games.

When a complete set of Virtuals had

returned to their game, the hatch of that game slammed shut.

The entire corridor rang out with footsteps. Hatches clanged shut.

"Where are you taking me?" asked Deezil in terror.

"Relax," smiled Max. "You're going to love it there."

Max rushed on down the corridor. He studied the signs above each hatch, very wary

that the portal was closing by the second.

He finally reached the sign he was looking for.

Deezil stared in horror at the sign. "No," he choked. "Please! Anywhere but here! I'm BEGGING YOU!"

The hatch for this game was already closed.

"You see," shouted Deezil. "You can't stick me in there! You'll have to return me to my home game."

Max reached into the pocket of his cargo pants and pulled out the Universal Hole Burner. He shone it against the hatch. With a fizzing sound, an opening appeared.

"Have fun!" grinned Max. He pulled Deezil out of the cage and flung him through the hole.

"NNNNNNNOOOOOOOOOOOOOOOOOO!!" screamed Deezil as he flew through the air.

A split second later, the hole closed up. Deezil's fate was sealed.

But there was no time for celebration. Soon the portal would be closed. He'd be stuck in here forever!

Max sped back through the hatch leading to *Slime Beasts of Death*. He hurtled through the undergrowth.

Please let the portal still be open!

Finally he reached the end of the trees. He pelted out into the field. He saw, to his horror, that the portal was almost closed.

He thundered across the field. His mind worked frantically on the dimensions of the portal. There was no way he'd be able to fit his whole body through the gap.

It would require something very special. A skill only he possessed.

As he crashed forward, he tucked his chin into his chest and wrapped up his body. He transformed himself into a human bowling ball. He closed his eyes and spun forward. To his amazement, his body crashed against the

sides of the portal as he flew through it.

Immediately, he heard a gigantic swooshing sound. The portal sealed up behind him.

He'd just made it.

He was back.

MAX FLASH MISSION 1

CHAPTER 21

Max was lying on the floor of a gloomy tunnel.
A rat was eyeing him with interest. He looked
all around. There was no sign of the portal
anywhere.

   To his left was a long metal ladder. It went
up toward a thin shaft of pale yellow light.
Stay down here and spend some quality
time with an inquisitive rodent? Or climb the
ladder?

   It wasn't a difficult decision.

   At the top of the ladder he discovered the

underside of a manhole. Using both hands, he pushed it up and to the left. He eased himself out. A car swerved out of his way. One of its wheels just missed Max's head.

For a second, he feared that he was still in the Virtual world and that this was *FX Turbo Racer*. But when he poked his head up, he saw

that he was smack in the middle of a very busy road. A very busy Gamer road.

A large bus bore down on him. Max rolled out of its way. He reached the sidewalk. He stood up and dusted himself off.

"Where did you come from?"

Max came face-to-face with a lanky policeman with thin lips and bushy eyebrows.

"From that manhole over there," Max replied, pointing to the middle of the road.

The policeman frowned. "Are you trying to be funny?" he asked.

Max turned around.

There was no sign of the manhole.

"So, where have you been?" asked the officer, leaning suspiciously toward him.

"It's complicated," said Max cautiously. "But I won't be going there again."

"And why is that then?"

"It was incredibly hard getting back from there. In fact, it was *virtually* impossible."

And with that Max flashed his cheesiest school-photograph smile and hurried off down the street. He hadn't got far when a blur of red and gold flashed before his eyes.

CHAPTER 22

Max tensed every muscle in his body. But he laughed out loud when he saw that the red and gold was just a leaf that had fallen from a tree. Two women passed by pushing strollers. When they saw him laughing at a leaf, they began whispering to each other and gave him strange looks. He walked on.

"Max!" cried his mom when she opened the front door. She smothered him with a big hug. His dad ran out of the kitchen, grinning widely.

"What a relief," whispered Dad. He placed a

strong arm around Max's shoulders.

"It's so good to be back," grinned Max.

"We want to hear all about it," beamed Mom. "But first you need to have your debrief with Zavonne."

His dad went with him down to the cellar. He moved the workbench and opened the floor panel.

"Aren't you coming with me?" asked Max.

His dad shook his head. "It was fine for us to be with you on the initial brief. But now that you're a full-fledged agent, you must meet with Zavonne on your own."

Max shrugged. "Cool," he said with a nod.

"Good," smiled his dad. "Have the debrief. Then come and tell us everything."

Max hurried down the metal ladder. He couldn't wait for Zavonne to applaud his efforts. Maybe she'd give him a reward, like a brand new computer with every Nexus Scope game.

Thirty seconds later, Max was back in the

communications center.

He pressed the green button he'd watched his mom press when he first came down here. The plasma screen sprang to life.

Zavonne's face appeared.

Max waited for her praise.

"What took you so long?" Zavonne demanded.

Max frowned. Was she joking? He'd just saved the human race from being trapped

inside the Virtual world. And she was being picky about his timing?

"I did it as fast as I could," he replied defensively.

"I take it you used all three gadgets?" asked Zavonne.

Max nodded.

Zavonne tutted.

"I only used them when my life was in danger," Max replied.

This was true, apart from using the Universal Hole Burner on the hatch. But how would Zavonne ever know?

"Overall," she noted, "your first mission was satisfactory."

Satisfactory? Was that the best she could do?

"I have a question," Max said.

Zavonne nodded.

"How did the portal close?"

Zavonne looked back at him coolly. "Our IT

people finally found a way to do it."

Max stared back at her in horror.

"But I was still in there!"

"It was a risk we had to take."

Even as she was saying this, something else occurred to Max. "Hang on a second. I think I've just worked out what EP-NR stands for. Those are the letters on the hub for Ricky's hard drive."

Zavonne stared at him without expression.

"It's ENTRY POINT—NO RETURN, isn't it?" said Max. "It must be. You sent me there on a one-way ticket!"

"Yes," conceded Zavonne. "That is what the letters stand for. But I had absolute faith in you. I knew that you would be able to make your way back to our world. That's why I allowed the use of the EP-NR hub. That's why I gave the go-ahead for our people to close the portal."

Max was absolutely stunned.

Zavonne had taken huge risks with his life.

Yet it didn't seem to faze her at all. Zavonne was unreal. She couldn't be human. She had the emotions of an ice sculpture.

"Right then," said Zavonne. "This debrief is over and—"

"Hang on a sec," blurted out Max. "What about the future? How do you know Ricky Stevens or some other programmer isn't going to accidentally create another portal?"

Zavonne looked at Max impatiently. "It was, as I told you, a one-in-one-billion accident. It will not happen again. And anyway, we now have the technical knowledge to close portals."

Max would have liked to ask her more questions. But Zavonne spoke again. "Our paths may meet again, Max," she said. She gave him a thin, impenetrable smile that was harder to crack than the Mona Lisa's. Then her face suddenly vanished from the screen.

Max's parents were waiting for him in the kitchen.

"We can't wait to hear about the mission," said his mom. "But first, you have to take a bath. You're absolutely filthy."

"I can't be," protested Max. "The DFEA clothes are self-cleaning. You heard what Zavonne said."

"It's not the clothes," laughed his dad. "It's your face. And what is that disgusting stuff in your hair?"

"Oh that," sighed Max. "It's probably Slime Beast drool."

He ran upstairs to the bathroom.

Typical!

He'd just saved the entire human race, and here were his parents treating him like a kid again!

EPILOGUE

Ricky Stevens had spent much of the weekend thinking about Deezil's disappearance from *Slime Beasts of Death*. He got to work early on Monday morning, determined to get to the bottom of the mystery. But as he entered the Programmers' Den, his boss asked him to take a look at *Farmyard Frolics*. She wanted to get his ideas about new features for the second version of the game.

Ricky grimaced. *Farmyard Frolics* wasn't a real game in his eyes. But it was best to keep his boss happy. He slid down onto his chair. He flicked on his computer and opened *Farmyard Frolics*.

As the game loaded, the wide-angle shot of the farm appeared. Ricky was stunned by what he saw.

There was Daisy Do-Good. She was supervising one of her workers whose job it was to go around the farm picking up the sheep droppings and loading them into a trash bag. The worker was covered from head to toe in sheep dung.

The worker was Deezil.

Ricky was just about to put Deezil back in *Slime Beasts of Death*. Then he paused and laughed out loud. Deezil looked so miserable. Maybe he'd leave him on the farm as punishment for his disappearing act. A few hours with dippy Daisy would tame even the most fearsome of lizard men.

GAME ON

Major thanks to
Jane Harris and
Lauren Buckland
for their massive
roles in creating Max
and their supreme
editing skills,
Monty Bhatia
for totally backing
this project from
the start,
Janice Swanson
for getting me in
on the "ground floor,"
and
Steph Thwaites
for always
being on the case.

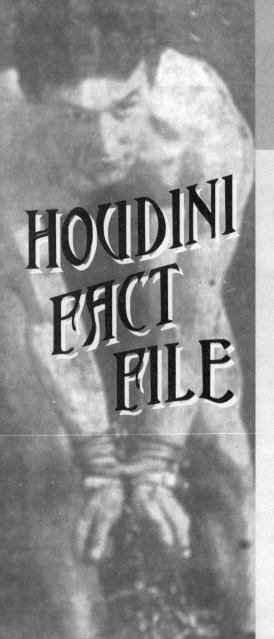

HOUDINI FACT FILE

Max's escape from a tank of water was based on one of Harry Houdini's most famous acts. This was known as the Chinese Water Torture Cell. It was first performed in 1913. The setup for this feat was in four stages. First, Houdini's feet were locked in stocks. Then he was suspended in midair from his ankles and had a restraint brace (similar to a straightjacket) fixed over his body. He was lowered headfirst into a steel-and-glass tank. The tank was called the "cell." It was completely filled with

THE CHINESE WATER TORTURE CELL

water. The restraint brace was locked to the roof of the
cell. And the cell lid was locked shut. As soon as the
lid was closed, a curtain was pulled across in front of
the cell so that the audience couldn't see what Houdini
was doing. Loud music played so they couldn't hear
anything either. Houdini was a master at keeping his
escape methods a secret. But magic experts insist they
know how he got out. They say that:

Houdini could hold his breath for three minutes.
(This feat should NEVER be tried by anyone except
the world's top escape artists). To escape from the
cell, Houdini had to unlock the stocks and the lock
tying his brace to the roof of the tank. To do this he
used a tiny key. This was either hidden in a miniscule,
impossible-to-spot pocket in the restraint brace, or he'd
swallowed a key and regurgitated it once inside the cell
(urgh!). To loosen the brace, Houdini used a special
technique where he puffed out his shoulders and chest
and then suddenly twisted his shoulders and wriggled
free. As for the cell's lid, this either had a false panel,
or it contained a secret lock—the key came in handy
for this, of course! Houdini then climbed out of the
cell and pulled the curtain aside. He was drenched in
water but alive. And audiences all over the world went
completely wild!

MONSTER SIGHTED!
OPINIONS WANTED!

posted by Coda:

Seventy-year-old Horace Winthrop has contacted us with a very suspicious story.

Mr. Winthrop was waiting for his grandson at Waterloo Station yesterday morning when he asserts that he was attacked by a terrifying red-and-gold lizard creature. There was total chaos as everyone tried to escape from the beast, which vanished when the police arrived.

Not an everyday occurrence, that's for sure.

A vicious monster causing carnage would be front-page news. Right? But there has been NO mention of this incident, and there appear to be no other witnesses.

Mr. Winthrop's memory of the event is very hazy, but he is convinced that it happened—

and that there are shady forces at work trying
to hush it up.

But WHY?

Faced with the usual firm denials from the
police, we come to the conclusion that this
episode was part of a secret police experiment
that went badly wrong. For years we have
been warning that the police are developing
new and sinister ways of fighting crime,
including the kind of robot we believe Mr.
Winthrop encountered. We think this machine
malfunctioned and the police panicked.
Regular readers of this website will know that
we are convinced that the police routinely wipe
the memories of those who get too close to
uncovering the truth—this would explain Mr.
Winthrop's hazy recollection.

Is there anyone else out there who can shed
any light on this incident? We want to hear
from YOU!

A SHORT TIME LATER,
ZAVONNE BRIEFS MAX
ON HIS SECOND TOP
SECRET MISSION . . .